A Note to Parents and Caregivers:

Read-it! Readers are for children who are just starting on the amazing road to reading. These beautiful books support both the acquisition of reading skills and the love of books.

 The PURPLE LEVEL presents basic topics and objects using high frequency words and simple language patterns.

 The RED LEVEL presents familiar topics using common words and repeating sentence patterns.

 The BLUE LEVEL presents new ideas using a larger vocabulary and varied sentence structure.

 The YELLOW LEVEL presents more challenging ideas, a broad vocabulary, and wide variety in sentence structure.

 The GREEN LEVEL presents more complex ideas, an extended vocabulary range, and expanded language structures.

 The ORANGE LEVEL presents a wide range of ideas and concepts using challenging vocabulary and complex language structures.

When sharing a book with your child, read in short stretches, pausing often to talk about the pictures. Have your child turn the pages and point to the pictures and familiar words. And be sure to reread favorite stories or parts of stories.

There is no right or wrong way to share books with children. Find time to read with your child, and pass on the legacy of literacy.

Adria F. Klein, Ph.D.
Professor Emeritus
California State University
San Bernardino, California

Editor: Jill Kalz
Designer: Lori Bye
Page Production: Melissa Kes
Art Director: Nathan Gassman
Associate Managing Editor: Christianne Jones
The illustrations in this book were created digitally.

Picture Window Books
151 Good Counsel Drive
P.O. Box 669
Mankato, MN 56002-0669
877-845-8392
www.picturewindowbooks.com

Printed in the United States of America.

All books published by Picture Window Books
are manufactured with paper containing at least
10 percent post-consumer waste.

Library of Congress Cataloging-in-Publication Data
Shaskan, Trisha Speed, 1973-
The fairies' first flight / by Trisha Speed Shaskan ; illustrated by Jisun Lee.
p. cm. — (Read-it! readers: tongue twisters)
ISBN-13: 978-1-4048-4875-7 (library binding)
[1. Tongue twisters—Fiction. 2. Fairies—Fiction. 3. Flight—Fiction.]
I. Lee, Jisun, ill. II. Title.
PZ7.S53242Fai 2008
[E]—dc22
                                        2008006337

The Fairies' First Flight

by Trisha Speed Shaskan
illustrated by Jisun Lee

Special thanks to our reading adviser:

Adria F. Klein, Ph.D.
Professor Emeritus, California State University
San Bernardino, California

PICTURE WINDOW BOOKS
Minneapolis, Minnesota

Flick and Flack were best friends.

Flick liked to fan and flutter her wings. She had the finest wings.

Flack's wings weren't as fine as Flick's. He could only flip-flop.

It was Flick and Flack's first year at flying school.
On Friday, Miss Freefall asked the fairies, "Are
you in tip-top shape?"

"Yes!" the fairies said.

"Fabulous! Then you're almost ready to fly!"
said Miss Freefall.

"Fan, flutter," thought Flick.

"Flip-flop," thought Flack.

"First, you need to figure out the magical phrase," said Miss Freefall.

"The phrase is made up of three things. First is the way your wings move. Second is what happens when you say the words fast. And third is the shape you have to be in to fly!"

"Let's figure out the phrase!" the fairies said.
Then all of the fairies fled.

Some fairies fled to the kitchen. Some fled down the hallway. Flick and Flack fled to the flower field.

"First, we need to figure out the way our wings move," said Flick.

Flack flapped his wings. "Flip-flop," he said.

Flick flapped her wings. "Fan, flutter," she said.

"Now we need to say the words fast," said Flick.

"Flip-flop," said Flack.

"Faster!" said Flick.

"Flip-flop, flip-flop, flip-flop," said Flack.

"Flack!" said Flick with a frown. "You're spitting and sputtering!"

"That's it!" said Flack. "It's the second clue. It's what happens when you say the words fast!"

"Fan, flutter, spit, sputter!" said Flick.

"Yes!" said Flack. "Flip-flop, spit, sputter."

And with that, Flick and Flack lifted into the air.
But they fell fast.

"What shape do you have to be in to fly?" asked Flack.

"Tip-top!" said Flick. "Flying is hard!"

"Flip-flop, spit, sputter, tip-top," said Flack.

"Fan, flutter, spit, sputter, tip-top," said Flick.

Flick and Flack both floated. But they fell fast.

"Fan, flutter," sighed Flick.

"Flip-flop," sighed Flack.

Then together they said, "Spit, sputter, tip-top."

The fairies lifted a few feet, floated, and flew!
Flick's wings fanned and fluttered. Flack's wings
flip-flopped. Flick and Flack felt light as feathers.

"That's it!" said Flack. "We needed to fan, flutter, *and* flip-flop."

"Fan, flutter, flip-flop, spit, sputter, tip-top! Fan, flutter, flip-flop, spit, sputter, tip-top!" they said.

Flick and Flack flew back inside.

"Fan, flutter, flip-flop, spit, sputter, tip-top! Fan, flutter, flip-flop, spit, sputter, tip-top!" they said over and over.

Miss Freefall nearly fainted. "Flick and Flack, that was fast!" she said.

"We worked together," said Flick.

"Fantastic," said Miss Freefall. "Have fun on your first fairy flight!"

More *Read-it!* Readers

Bright pictures and fun stories help you practice your reading skills. Look for more books at your level.

Alex and the Team Jersey
Alex and Toolie
Another Pet
Betty and Baxter's Batter Battle
The Big Pig
Camden's Game
Cass the Monkey
Charlie's Tasks
Flora McQuack
Harold Hickok Had the Hiccups
Lady Lulu Liked to Litter

Marconi the Wizard
Peppy, Patch, and the Bath
Peter's Secret
Pets on Vacation
The Princess and the Tower
Sausages!
Theodore the Millipede
The Three Princesses
Tromso the Troll
Willie the Whale
The Zoo Band

On the Web

FactHound offers a safe, fun way to find Web sites related to topics in this book. All of the sites on FactHound have been researched by our staff.

1. Visit *www.facthound.com*

2. Type in this special code:
   1404848754

3. Click on the FETCH IT button.

Your trusty FactHound will fetch the best sites for you!
A complete list of *Read-it!* Readers is available on our Web site:
www.picturewindowbooks.com

24